EVERYDAY LESSONS #1

Disney
FROZEN

HOORAY FOR DIFFERENCES!

A Random House PICTUREBACK® Book
Random House 🏠 New York

© 2022 Disney Enterprises, Inc. All rights reserved. Published in the United States by Random House Children's Books,
a division of Penguin Random House LLC, 1745 Broadway, New York, NY 10019, and in Canada by Penguin Random House Canada
Limited, Toronto, in conjunction with Disney Enterprises, Inc. Pictureback, Random House, and the Random House colophon
are registered trademarks of Penguin Random House LLC.
rhcbooks.com
ISBN 978-0-7364-4278-7 (trade)
Printed in the United States of America
10 9 8 7 6 5 4 3 2 1

"I can't wait to see my little brothers!" Olaf exclaimed. He, Anna, Elsa, Kristoff, and Sven were headed to the ice palace. That was where Olaf's brothers lived. "First, I'll hug Sludge and Slush and Slide. Then Flake and Crystal and Fridge . . ."

Olaf stopped naming his little brothers and started to think of a fun activity to do with them.

"Oooh, I know!" he said, clapping his hands. "Maybe Sven can take us for a ride, and we can go exploring! My brothers love exploring, just like me!"

The friends continued up the mountain
until they reached the ice palace steps.

"We're almost there!" Olaf said happily.
"I'm so EXCITED! I bet my
brothers will be excited, too!
Just wait till they see me!"

At the top of the stairs, Olaf burst through the huge
front doors and spread his little twiggy arms wide.
   "Surprise, little brothers! I'm here!" he shouted.
"Group hug!"
   But Olaf's brothers were too busy to notice him.

Suddenly, one of the snowgies sailed through
the air, landing on top of Olaf!

"Oh, hi there, little Slush!" Olaf said.

"Do you know what you need?" he asked the snowgie. "A carrot nose like mine! Don't worry! I've got you covered."

Olaf took one of Sven's carrots out of their picnic basket. But when he tried to give it to Slush, the snowgie ran away!

"WAIT! COME BACK!" Olaf called.

He tried to catch two other snowgies.

"Do you want a hug?" he called out hopefully, but they ran right past him.

"Olaf?" Elsa asked gently. "Are you all right?"

"Yeah," he answered. "But I thought my brothers would like warm hugs, just like me."

"It's okay to be different—" Anna started to say.

"But my brothers love to spend time with family, just like me!" Olaf insisted.

Several snowgies scurried noisily across the floor. CRASH! They knocked Olaf right over! This was not how he had imagined family fun time at all.

Olaf looked around at all his pieces on the floor, then quietly said, "Hmm. Maybe my brothers don't like the same things I do."

"Oh, Olaf," Anna said while she and Elsa put him back together. "It's okay if we're different from others in our family."

"It's true," Elsa added. "Just look at Anna and me!"

"I like to sleep late," Anna explained, "but Elsa likes to get up early. Really early!"

"And Anna's favorite season is summer, while mine is winter," Elsa said.

"But we appreciate each other, including our differences," Anna explained. "I can still enjoy winter things with Elsa."

"And I can still enjoy summer things with Anna," Elsa said, grinning.

"We always love and look out for each other," Anna said, giving the snowman a hug. "You see, Olaf—no matter what, we're sisters."

"Yes, we're **FAMILY**!" Elsa agreed. "And that family includes you, too!"

"I get it!" Olaf said, smiling. He paused and added, "I think."
A few snowgies sped by. Elsa pointed to them and said,
"Sometimes your little brothers like to race around, but . . ."
"I sometimes like to glide and pivot!" Olaf finished happily.

Anna and Elsa laughed. They went on to point out that the snowgies were even different from each other! At that moment, some were playing happily. Some looked tired. Some were being silly, and others looked confused.

"Differences make life more FUN!" Anna said.

"And interesting," Elsa added.

"Yeah, my family certainly makes my life more fun and interesting," Kristoff said.

"That's right!" Olaf said. "Your family is Sven and the trolls, and you're all so different from each other!"

"Oh, look!" Olaf pointed toward the open doors. "It's snowing!"

The friends walked outside to enjoy the gentle snowfall.

"I think you understand better than you realize," Elsa said. "Each snowflake is unique and special—just like you and your little brothers."

Olaf gasped in delight. "They're all DIFFERENT, just like us!"

The snowgies and Marshmallow began gathering around Olaf.
"Hey, little brothers, do you like the snowflakes?" Olaf asked.
The snowgies and Marshmallow nodded.
"That's great!" Olaf said. "Each one is different and special, but
they all belong together—just like all of us!"

"Let's make snow angels!" Elsa suggested.

"Let's have a snowball fight!" Anna cried.

"Let's have lunch!" Kristoff said.

Olaf and Marshmallow helped the snowgies go sledding.

"It's okay. We can all do something different!" Olaf said.

"But we'll do it TOGETHER!"